# DISNEY
# ALICE
## *in*
## WONDERLAND
## A Snack for the Queen

AUTUMN PUBLISHING

It was a lovely day
in Wonderland. Alice
was sitting in a garden,
watching the bread-
and-butterflies flitter
from flower to flower.

"Everything here in
Wonderland is so very
curious," sighed Alice.

Then, she heard a
voice behind her.

"Oh dear, oh dear,
oh dear!"

Alice turned to see the White Rabbit running through the garden. "Is everything all right?" she asked.

The White Rabbit stopped. "The Queen of Hearts is hungry, but nothing in the palace seems to satisfy her. If I don't find her a tasty treat soon, she'll have my head!"

"Perhaps I can help," Alice said. "I've never had any trouble finding something to eat in Wonderland. If we work together, I'm sure we will find something that makes the Queen happy."

"Have you tried asking the Mad Hatter?" Alice asked. "His tea table is always filled with treats."

"Oh, no. I try to steer clear of the Hatter," the White Rabbit replied. "He's always causing trouble."

"That's true," said Alice. Then she stopped short. "Look at these cupcakes! Perhaps we don't need the Mad Hatter after all."

Alice plucked a cupcake from the bush, and
she and the White Rabbit hurried to the palace.

"We brought you a cupcake, Your Majesty,"
she said, handing the Queen the treat.

But, before the Queen could take a bite, the cupcake
began to move. Two wings opened up, and it flew away.
It wasn't a cupcake at all. It was a bird!

Alice and the White Rabbit quickly ran from
the palace, sure that the Queen would have
their heads now! They hadn't gone far when the
Cheshire Cat appeared in front of them.
"What's the hurry?" he asked.

"We need to find a snack for the Queen," Alice replied.

"Take her some of these blue berries," the Cheshire Cat suggested.

"But some of those berries are red!" Alice said.

"I think you'll find that red is blue!" the cat grinned.

Puzzled, Alice picked some of the red berries, and took them to the Queen. The Queen was delighted when she spied the fruit, and eagerly reached out to pick one. She popped the berry in her mouth, and licked her lips with delight at its wonderful taste.

"Delicious!" cried the Queen. "These berries are quite unlike any I have ever tasted! They are simply divine! I suppose you may keep your heads after all!"

Alice and the White Rabbit sighed with relief, while the greedy Queen helped herself to another handful of the delicious red fruit.

But then the Queen noticed something: she had turned blue!
"Oh, dear," Alice said. "That must be why the Cheshire Cat said
that red is blue. The red berries turn you blue when you eat them!"
"Fix me!" the Queen yelled.

"I have an idea," Alice said, and rushed back to the berry bushes. This time, she picked some blue berries, then hurried to the Queen.

"Eat these!" Alice urged.

Scowling, the Queen ate some of the berries. Slowly, the blue faded from her skin.

"I suppose that worked," she huffed. "But I'm still hungry!"

As Alice and the White Rabbit hurried off to find another snack, they bumped into Tweedledum and Tweedledee. The twins were dancing and singing a silly song:

"When it comes to treats, we are not picky
We love a treat that's sweet and sticky!"

"Excuse me," said Alice. "We just happen to be looking for a tasty treat for the Queen. May we have a lollipop?"

"If it's for the Queen, we can't say no," said Tweedledum.

"So take a lollipop and off you go!" finished Tweedledee.

Alice gave the lollipop to the Queen.
"Hmmm," she said, as she licked the treat. "I do love lollipops!"
But then her face turned bright red with heat.
"Spicy! Spicy!" the Queen yelled. "Bring me some water!"

While the guards rushed to help the Queen, Alice and the White Rabbit fled.

"That's it! I'm going to find the Mad Hatter," Alice said. "I'm sure he will have a good snack for the Queen."

At the Mad Hatter's house, Alice found him serving tea to the March Hare.

"Excuse me," she said, "but the Queen of Hearts needs a snack. She's very hungry, and very cross. Can you help?"

The Mad Hatter grinned.
He handed a cookie to Alice.
"This is exactly what the
Queen needs," he promised.

So Alice and the White Rabbit brought the cookie to the Queen. She sniffed it suspiciously.

"It smells good," she said, frowning. "And it looks tasty."

Then the Queen frowned again, and glared at Alice. "Is it tasty, though?" she demanded.

"I am quite sure it is delicious," Alice said, clasping her hands and hoping that she was right. She had noticed that the Mad Hatter had quite a twinkle in his eye when he had handed her the cookie.

The Queen bit into the cookie.

"It is tasty!" she exclaimed.

She munched and munched happily. But suddenly, something very strange happened...

... the Queen began to shrink! She got smaller and smaller, until she was no bigger than the cookie itself.

"Oh, dear!" sighed Alice. "It seems that the Mad Hatter has been up to his old tricks again. That cookie was more than just a tasty snack!"

"My, oh, my! What will become of us now?" spluttered the White Rabbit. Alice stared at the queen with wide eyes as she stamped her feet and opened her mouth wide.

"Guards! Guards! Off with their heads!" the Queen yelled. But her voice was so tiny and squeaky that the guards didn't hear her.

Alice and the White Rabbit hurried away, chuckling. "Well, I have to agree with the Mad Hatter after all," Alice giggled. "That cookie is exactly what the Queen needed!"